Demonic Invasion

By Roofus P Fox

Cobalt Dog Press, LLC

Demonic Invasion
A Cobalt Dog Press Book

Contents

Disclaimer:

All characters appearing in this work are fictitious. Any resemblance to real persons, living or dead, is purely coincidental. This work is based on events taking place in a parallel universe, as such it is clearly fiction in our universe.

There are some names and events that are borrowed from our universe:

Example Sam Walton founder of Walmart, Jesse Ventura, etc.

In those select cases the use of such names and events surrounding them are "fair use". The reason is to show the similarity of the universe of this story to our own, and to set a basic framework for the story.

Chapter 1

Order of the Bookbag

February 1991

John was sitting in study-hall, writing a letter to the Principal of Western High school, asking why students are forbidden from carry their books in bookbags in the hallways between classes, when another student whispered to him.

"Hey John," Nelson said, "what are you writing?"

"A letter to the Principal about being able to carry bookbags in the hallways"

"Cool," Said Nelson, as he returned to his studies.

John sat there for a few minutes thinking. There he was all excited about this letter, and this other student just sort of shrugged it off. Something about that infuriated John to the point that writing a letter was not enough now.

The chairs in study-hall were plastic spring loaded ones where the seat automatically flipped up when someone was no longer sitting in them. As he stood up, throughout the hall a squeaking sound could be heard as the crap chair he was sitting in sprung back.

John Buck started walking to the Principal's office to speak with him about how things are at Western High School. He was very annoyed when upon standing up from his seat in study-hall, the seat made a loud squeaking noise. Walking out of the study-hall he began his journey to the main office. It was a long and fateful journey.

As he was walking down the hall he decided to enter the restroom, to use the toilet, as he always did before he was going to confront someone or do something he thought was important. After he flushed the urinal, suddenly all the urinals in the restroom started flushing simultaneously. At the same time a hole started opening up in the floor of the restroom. Stairs appeared. So, he started walking down the stairs, and noticed the floor resealing above him.

There was a hallway. It appeared to be of much older construction than the school above it. Along the old stone walls were what appeared to be cast iron rings about every 10 feet along the hallway. In those rings were lamps with lit flames burning some type of oil. Music was playing that he had never before heard in his life. It was the most beautiful music he ever heard. It was not until he reached the end that he really took notice as to how perfectly polished the black granite floor was.

At the end of the hallway was a solid oak door. Carved on it were symbols of books, above that was the words "Order of the Bookbag". Standing there in awe he suddenly heard the sound of hinges creaking as the door slowly opened. To his amazement, there was another hallway behind the door. This hallway was about twice as long as the first one. Along the walls were old paintings of students who have been dead for many years. At the end of the hall there was a second doorway. On one side of the doorway was what appeared to be an original copy of the declaration of independence of the united States of America. On the other side was the Constitution of the united States of America. Both were sealed in glass cases.

Beyond the doorway was a large room with shelves of books along three of the four walls. The wall at the far end had a bar complete with adjustable bar-stools. At the side of the bar was a standard size door.

"Mr Buck," said, a voice from behind the bar, "Samantha, is waiting for you in her office."

Samantha was John Buck's sponsor, and today was the fateful day to be initiated as a member of Order of the Bookbag. Samantha and John became acquainted soon after he started to attend Western High. Eventually they would share a passionate kiss, however that was the only kiss they ever shared and as far as they took their physical relationship. They would each remember that kiss, the rest of their lives.

Her office had book shelves along one of the walls. Along another wall was a glass case.

"Have a seat John," she said as she pointed at the chair on the side of the desk opposite hers.
After sitting down she asked if he was absolutely sure about going through with the initiation. She called another member to perform the actual initiation.

There are rumors, then there are rumors of rumors. Years ago a physics professor named Dr John Geiklan disappeared. Some say, he is dead. There were rumors that he left the USA and became a citizen of another nation. There were even rumors that he was part of a terrorist organization. It did not surprise John when he walked through the door.

Samantha put her hand on what appeared to be a simple paperweight on her desk. Presently, a concealed door about one foot square opened and a tray slid out from the wall. On the tray was a small assortment of cigarettes, a few cigars, and three glasses with drinks, complete with ice cubes. Dr

Geiklan lit one of the cigars and slowly took a few puffs from his cigar before he picked up his drink and sat down in his chair. Then Samantha stood up, walked over to the tray, picked up a cigarette and her drink, sitting back down at her desk. She lit her cigarette, took a healthy lung full of smoke and then took a sip of her drink, before she exhaled. John walked over picked up his glass and sat back down.

It was the glass of Dr Pepper from which all other Dr Peppers would be measured and found wanting. He was sitting there enjoying the taste when Dr Geiklan spoke for the first time since walking in the room.

"Mr Buck," he began, "we have been watching you for years."
"It has been determined by many who are learned in the study of psychology and personality, that you have a natural inborn resistance to negative propaganda, affecting the mind. Do you have any questions before we begin?"

"Can members of Order of the Bookbag carry bookbags in the hallways between classes?" John began, "How long until the bookbag ban is lifted?"

"If students of Western High are ever freely allowed to carry bookbags in the hallways, it will be many years in the future," he stated with the seriousness of a general, "Mr Buck, you will never carry a bookbag as a student in high school again."

"Then what purpose does Order of the Bookbag serve?" John responded.

"The real reason students are forbidden from carrying bookbags in the hallways is to prepare them to live in a totalitarian police state." Dr Geiklan began.
"As you already know, I have a PhD in physics and mathematics. I also look for patterns in history, the behavior of populations, sociology etc. It took me a few years of watching the trends to see the pattern emerge. When I realized what was happening, I resigned as professor of physics the following morning."

While Dr Geiklan was speaking, Samantha was slowing puffing on a cigarette and sipping her drink.

"Did you notice that the state is preparing to pass a law raising the legal age to purchase tobacco from 16 to 18?" Dr Geiklan continued, "I remember when the first law was passed requiring people to be 16 to legally purchase tobacco products."
"Haven't you ever wondered why the legal restrictions are always getting more restricted over time?"

"Why does the law never become less restricted?" "What do you think is more likely to happen in the future, the legal age to consume alcoholic beverages lowered from 21 to 18, or the legal age to purchase and smoke a cigarette raised from 18 to 21?" Dr Geiklan continued, "Those are rhetorical questions, everyone in this room already knows the answer."
"You regularly ready the news paper," He went on to drive the point home, "I'm sure you saw the story where the IRS accidentally overcharged someone."

"Did you ever see a story in the news about the IRS accidentally undercharging someone for taxes?"

"Of course you didn't," Dr Geiklan answered his own question before John could.

"If these things were accidents, then there would be some accidents in favor of the taxpayer. It can not be incompetence, because incompetence would bring a variety of results. Consistently negative results, indicates malice."

Dr Geiklan continued talking for many minutes. Every sentence hit John Buck's consciousness almost like a physical blow. Many of the questions and ideas Dr Geiklan spoke about were thoughts that John had but never shared before with anyone. As Dr Geiklan was speaking thoughts were exploding in John's mind, thoughts like:

Of Course! I always knew that in my heart!

Yes, it is true.

I thought I was the only one who saw these things.

".......and then I saw the undeniable truth and my knees buckled," Dr Geiklan now speaking barely above a whisper, "I had to put my hands on my desk to steady myself as I was standing there."

"What truth?" John asked.

"The government of the united States of America, along with every major government of the world has been infiltrated and taken over by people who worship the devil," he continued, "Their plan is to use the authority of the state

xi

and national governments around the world to enslave the human race."

"The ultimate goal of the demons possessing them, is the total annihilation and extinction of the human race, and if they can pull it off, the eventual extinction of all life on Earth."

"Order of the Bookbag was created to oppose them?" John asked.

"There are many organizations some more recently created, and some much older," Samantha spoke for the first time since Dr Geiklan arrived. "One of the main purposes that Order of the Bookbag was created for is to preserve knowledge, and real education. The purpose of schools today is to destroy the minds of the students and young people. Our mission is to spread the knowledge of this threat to the future of the human race to students that are ready to receive the message. It is also to inspire real learning."

"You see, John," she continued, "people especially young people have an innate curiosity about the world and how things work. People have a natural drive to learn new things. These government schools purpose is to make learning and education as painful as possible for young students, so they will turn against their own nature."

"A person who has been trained to shut their own mind down is more easily controlled and enslaved."

"Most people will never have an original thought in their life," Dr Geiklan, interjected.

The sad truth of the last statement hit John so hard, he closed his eyes for a few seconds barely being able to hold back his emotion.

They sat there and spoke until early afternoon. As he was sitting there John knew that he was going to be dropping out of school before the spring.

"After you leave this room we may not ever meet again," Dr Geiklan said, "Spend these next years learning, and exploring. Find a way to travel to different areas of the USA and even other countries if you can. While you are doing this, keep your eyes and ears open. However, know that silence is your friend."
As John walked out of the room, he was now a member of Order of the Bookbag. He was 16 years old,

same age as Samantha. He saw her a few times before he dropped out of high school a few months later. After that he would only see her once more in his life, and sadly it would take many years until he realized just how rare a lady of intelligence and wisdom is, especially with beauty.

A few days later it was time for John Buck's lunch period at the high school. There was a library across the hall from the cafeteria. He decided to use his lunch time to study and do some research at the library. This was the first and last time he would enter the school library.

The library of Western High school was at the top of a winding set of stairs. It was about the size of an average high school library. A few feet from the door there was a counter with a librarian sitting behind doing things that librarians do. There were some tables and chairs right next to the counter. While the library itself seemed to have the standard layout like the ones in his other school, John noticed two differences. There were no other students in there studying or readying. And the tables he saw were pushed up much closer to the librarian's counter.

John spent some time at the bookshelves looking for a book to read. There was two small desks with chairs near the end of one of the bookshelves at the far end of the library. John sat down and started to read his book.

"What are you doing back there?" The librarian-cop was speaking loudly, just below a shout.

"Reading a book," John replied after recovering from the shock of a librarian talking to him in a hateful tone of voice in a library.

"COME HERE," the librarian-Nazi said, louder still, almost shouting.

Now, John stands up and walks out toward the librarian counter. At this point he is confused and is trying not to let total shock show on his face.

"If you want to read a book," she said, "you must sit down there." As she was making the statement she was pointing at one of the tables pushed up next to her counter.

"Then why are desks and chairs over there," John point back where he was, "where I was sitting reading a book?"
xiv

"You must sit there so I can watch you," she snarled with a face filled with such hate, that she looked like the Emperor trying to kill Luke Skywalker in Return of the Jedi.

John immediately walked out of the library. It was clear now, why there were no students studying at the library. The other students of the school must find it just as difficult to study sitting next to a hate filled demon. That is why they avoided the library.

Chapter 2

Flashback to 1980s

At the end of each December the extended family of John Buck would gather for an afternoon feast. There were usually 2 or 3 such gatherings a year. Usually the event would take place at one of John's grandparent's houses. Throughout his childhood he experienced this tradition. Aunts, Uncles, cousins, and such would arrive during the late morning and once everyone was there, they would all sit down to a big feast. After the feast, the family would usually gather into 3 groups.

First there would be the men sitting around discussing, business, politics, philosophy, and sometimes sports.

Then there were the children running around doing what children do.

The third group were the gossiping women.

Now because John was naturally curious, as the years passed, he would spent less and less time with the children and more time with the adults. He usually split the time between the women and the men, listening to what they have to say.

It was much easier for him to make sense of what the men were talking about, than the musings of the women.

The women would talk about who died within the last year, people getting sick, babies being born, people getting married. They would usually start speaking about real people, some of whom John recognized the names. Then suddenly without warning the their conversations would get bizarre, speaking about people cheating and strange things.

".......Oh I missed last week's show, so I didn't realize she was cheating on Roger with that hunk," Sally was saying.

SHOW? They are talking about a TV show!

It was so bizarre to John. These women suddenly were talking about people on a TV show. They would gossip about real people and events, then suddenly with no warning they would be talking about artificial characters in a TV show, as if they were just as real.

These were old traditions that were slowly fading away. John's childhood was in the 1980s when there was still a greater residual inertia of wealth and family bonds still in existence in America. As he got older he noticed a subtle shift in what the adults were speaking about.

The men would speak of some future danger, of some threat to the nation and culture.

"....... and the big corporations are merging to crush the middle class," Fredrick was saying.

"Yes, it looks like the blue color working man is in trouble..........."

".......there could be a war......"

Sometimes John would hear such talk from the women, but it was much more rare, and when they did speak that way it was religious based. Women mostly gossiped.

The last few years of his childhood as he was preparing to become a man, he began to notice a different attitude emanating from the women in some of the conversations he overheard.

"Men are so lucky," Ethel spoke, "they have it so easy."
xix

"They have the best jobs and get paid more money," Rachel added.

These type of statements were confusing to John, because he never noticed any advantages to being a boy. It would be awesome when he got older and could enjoy the extra privileges of being a man, he had heard women speaking about.

Chapter 3

Trash Landfill

March 1996

As the power and ownership of business became more concentrated into fewer people the actual wages paid to entry level workers steadily declined. Instead of hiring people directly, many business started using more and more temporary workers, hired through temporary employment companies. The main purpose of the temporary employment companies were to manage the labor surplus.

Now after the layoff at the warehouse, John Buck found himself working for a temporary employment company. He would be sent out to various business to work for a week or two. Sometimes the job or assignment would only last a day. The ones that lasted a day it was usually because someone at the business did not like the way he looked. They would usually tell him at the end of the day not to return, however, many times they did not have the honor to tell him to his face. Many times John would return to his place and find a message on his answering machine, telling him the assignment is over. He would call the temporary company about once a day asking if they had another assignment for him. And so it went for him awhile.

One day in February the temporary service sent him to a landfill. He remained at the landfill as he saved money for the plans to build a robot dog and as he moved forward with his political plans.

He started to seek out others who had the same beliefs in liberty. Up until this point John only knew of the two major political parties, Republican and Democrat. The republicans recently won the majority in congress and most States for the first time in about 40 years. Hence, for the first time in his life the democrats were not the controlling party.

During the last few years that the democrats held power, the republicans would speak of freedom, liberty, reducing the size of government. This was something that appealed to the vast majority of the younger people, especially John Buck.

And it so happened that he joined the Republican party when he became old enough to register to vote.

However, the only major thing that the republicans did once they became the majority party, was repeal the federal 55 mph speed-limit on interstate highways. Most people didn't notice any other reduction in federal regulations. Many people were beginning to realize that if they were going to see an increase in liberty, something else was needed.

Now John did not discuss politics, or much else when he first started working at the landfill. His first duties there were walking around the place looking for things out of the ordinary. Sometimes he would be assigned various things to do. Sometimes he got to go out with a trash truck to pick up garbage to bring back to the landfill.

"Who started this landfill?" John asked one day as they were out on a garbage run.

"His name is Borace Mingela," John answered, "Sometimes he can be seen waiting near his mailbox at the end of his driveway."

"He waits for his mail everyday?"

"Not everyday, usually we only see him out waiting around the first week of the month"

"Really?"

"The check he gets from the landfill lease is sent to him right after the 1st business day of the month."

"Lease?" John was puzzled, "You mean the land is not owned by the landfill company?"

"About 60 percent of the actual land that we put the trash on is owned by the landfill company, the other 40 percent, we must lease from Mr Mingela."

"Did Mr Mingela ever offer to sell the land to the company?"

"No, in fact some of our best negotiators tried to get him to sell those acres," John said, "Mingela refuses to sell."

"That makes no sense at all," John stated, "Why would anyone turn down the option to transfer the liability of owning land with massive amounts of waste?"

"Old man Mingela says that he doesn't want to give up those lease payments."

On this day they pulled up to a location with a large pile of stuff. They loaded the stuff into the trash truck until only the piano was left. Yes that's right, someone was actually throwing out a full size upright piano.

"This piano is going to be difficult to load into the back," Steve said.

Steve and John were the 2 loaders who were doing most of the pick ups. John was driving.

"All we need is a sledgehammer," John said trying not laugh.

"I got one in the truck," John was already opening up the side compartment that the sledgehammer.

John was disappointed to see John hand Steve the sledgehammer, because he was really looking forward to smashing a piano. Perhaps some other day he will have the opportunity to smash a piano. Perhaps Steve will only smash it partially and let John do some damage.

Steve brought the sledgehammer down so forcefully that the piano exploded into pieces with his first hit. John would not share in the piano destruction that day.

Months passed, winter became spring, grass and weeds started to grow around the landfill. John would run a mower and other equipment as needed around the landfill. Sometimes his duties took him to houses that were on the border of the landfill itself.

By the time John started working at the landfill, it had expanded to the point where it was overtaking surrounding houses. In years past the company that owned the landfill would buy up as much of the surrounding properties as possible. Then they would simply expand the landfill onto those places. This is why they now owned about 60 percent of the landfill property, with Borace Mingela's share down to 40 percent. In the beginning Mingela's share was 100 percent. Throughout the years as the landfill bought out other surrounding farms, Mingela's share shrank as a percentage.

On one fateful day John and Steve were sent to an old farmhouse. Their job was to clean it out, because the landfill was about to expand over that area. The company wanted to salvage anything of value that may be inside the building before it was demolished.

As John explored the building he stumbled upon what appeared to be a concealed room. It was not possible to access this room in the conventional way. It was about a half floor above the main level. There were no stairs leading to it. If it were not for his natural curiosity he would have shut the closet door and walked away after making sure there was nothing of value inside. But, there was something different about this closet. This closet was higher than the other rooms of the main floor by about 2 feet. Also on the inner most side were boards
spaced about as far apart as a standard ladder. The ladder ended about 2 and a half feet from the ceiling.

John looked around to make sure no one was looking as he shut the closet door behind him. The hidden panel was easy to open. On the other side the floor was about 3 feet below, and there were stairs.

It appeared to be some special office. In the center was a desk and a chair. As he sat down in the chair John Buck looked around. On one of the walls there was an old painting of George Washington. He was wearing what appeared to be a bib or apron. On the apron was a design containing 3 main elements, a carpenter's square, an architect's compass, and the capital letter G. On another wall there was an old black & white picture.

John carefully searched the drawers of the desk.. The desk itself was designed down to the minimum utility of what a desk was used for. The top was a sanded smooth oak finish. There were 3 drawers on each side and a single thin wide drawer between them. Beneath the center drawer was an open space for the user's legs and feet. All sides of the desk were flat and at 90 degree angles.

All of the drawers were empty, save two. The center contained 2 pens, 1 pencil, 5 paperclips, 1 eraser, and a pair of glasses in a leather case. In the bottom right drawer was an old book. Beneath the book there was a cigar box. John opened the book to find out it was printed in 1885. The cigar box contained a key, a map, and a piece of paper with a list of names. One of those names was Borace Mingela.

John walked over to get a closer look at the old black & white picture on the wall. The picture was of three men standing in the middle of a field. Each of them had a shovel. All three shovels had wooden handles, and the metal digging part was rounded with a sharp point, for breaking ground. Under the picture was a brass plaque, with an inscription written thereon.

"On this day February 2, 1962 ground was broken on a new landfill by Roger Natz, William Black, and Borace Mingela."

John put the book and cigar box in a bag as he vacated the room.

"I thought you disappeared," Steve started speaking when he next saw John.

"I was busy cleaning out a closet."

John walked over to the truck and tossed the bag behind his seat.

"What is in the bag?"

"Just an old book."

It has been John's experience that most people put little or no value on books. He was sure he would be allowed to keep it, even if he had to show it to someone to prove it was just a book. Of course the cigar box was not mentioned.

Later when John was alone at his house he opened the cigar box to examine the map. Perhaps this is a treasure map. As he did this, he had the television on, tuned to the national news. The map itself appeared to be of the landfill.

".........and other news it was 4 years ago today that Sam Walton, founder of Walmart died......."

There were areas on the map that he remembered seeing as he worked at various places around the landfill. He made plans to explore the areas on the map. There could be a hidden treasure of some type. He remember some of people who worked at the landfill for a few years tell him that they sometimes find cash, even once found thousands of dollars in one day.

"............*is leading in the pols against Bob Dole.............Clinton should easily win reelection.........*"

That night John dreamed he was President of the united States of America and great mall in the center of Washington DC was turned into a landfill.

On his days off from the landfill, John would do work to advance his political plans. Sometimes he would go to the local town meeting to learn about what really happens at a meeting. Most times he would see the president or a vice president of the landfill company attending the meeting. They would say hello to John, and perhaps talk shop. At the latest meeting, the town board was debating expansion plans for the landfill. Now part of those plans included the construction of a waste to energy electric generator. Everyone in the room knew that this meeting and debate were merely formalities. Too much money was flowing into the right pockets to stop this train.

For some reason John never saw Borace Mingela at a meeting, sometimes one of his lawyers would make an

appearance, or even one of his family members, but never Mr Mingela himself. About the only time people saw him was the first week of the month when he waits for his check by his mailbox. Even with all that money he still chose to live in his old farmhouse across the street from the landfill.

On most spots on the old map, John would find nothing of significance. He was about to toss the map into the fireplace when he realized there was one place on the map he never fully explored. However, the reason he never explored that location happens to be because it is outside the boundaries of the landfill.

Across the street from the northern end of the landfill is an old school building. This school building was the kind that are depicted in old paintings of schoolhouses from the 1870s. It had the standard slanted peaked roof, with a chimney for a fireplace or wood-stove heater.

"John, I have a question," John began, "Were you ever in that old schoolhouse?"

"Nope"

"Do you know of anyone who's been inside it?"

"I don't know of anyone going inside it since the landfill company tried to purchase the property about 5 years ago."

"Who owns the schoolhouse?"

"The land and schoolhouse is owned by a trust. This trust is overseen of a board of trustees and one of the trustees is Borace Mingela."

Chapter 4

Gateway to Parallel Worlds

"Are you sure you want to do this?"

"I have to do this," John answered.

"Ok, once you get out of the car," Jason spoke in a serious tone, "you are on your own."

It was just before midnight when they started driving past the landfill property. John was wearing a dark sweatshirt with a hood pulled around his head and a dark cloth over his face. Sitting in the passenger of Jason's car if it was possible to see the look on his face, it would be the look of inescapable determination. He had to see what was contained inside that schoolhouse, no matter what the cost. Even if losing his life was the price he had to pay, he was going to find out what was hidden there.

"What the hell?" Jason had just noticed some large 18 wheelers with lights on near the edge of the landfill.

"There is not suppose to be activity in the landfill at night," John was saying, "In fact they usually close the gate before 8pm."

"That activity is at the other side of the landfill, so they shouldn't notice me stopping for a few seconds to drop you off near the school."

"Yeah, it looks like all their attention is focused at the southwest corner of the landfill."
The men who were unloading the equipment off the trucks were flown in by private jet 12 hours ago. No one within 500 miles had ever seen these men before. Standing next to a Lincoln town-car was a man wearing a dark suit watching the men unload and carry the equipment into a building that was constructed within the last hour. Sometimes one of the men who were working would walk up to the man in the suit. A few words would be exchanged and then he would go back to working with the other men while the man in the suit

XXXV

continued to watch. Since he wearing a fedora, the only thing people could see from a distance about his face was a partially graying beard and a cigar. Suddenly one of the men started walking fast, almost running toward the man in the suit.

"Dr Konavich," William was talking in a hushed tone just above a whisper, as was standard protocol, "a car was spotted stopping momentarily near the schoolhouse."

As William walked back to the truck, Dr Konavich pulled a phone out of an inner suit pocket. He slowly pulled the cigar out of his month as he dialed a phone number.

Jason decided to stop at a tavern and have a glass of whiskey on the rocks after dropping John Buck off near the school. He rarely drinks any alcoholic beverages, much less hard whiskey, but he needed it tonight. He sat down at the bar and ordered a glass of single-malt scotch on the rocks.

John didn't bother with the front door of the schoolhouse. He walked around the back and found a smaller backdoor. In less than a min he was walking through the doorway. There were a number of desks and chairs in the building. One of the desks was about 3 times larger than the rest. Near the large desk was a leather chair. In the center of the room stood a wood-stove. The stove had a pipe that connected to a stone chimney. This chimney had to be almost 4 feet in diameter.

It only took John a minute to realize the chimney did not fit in with the rest of the building. He knew there was no way the simple wooden floor could hold the weight of the chimney. He began to closely examine the chimney on all sides. Then about 3 feet from the floor on the side opposite the stove he found what he was looking for.

He pulled the old key out of the cigar box and slowly inserted it into the matching pattern in the stone. At first he wasn't sure if it would work, because it would not turn. He increased the pressure slightly and suddenly there was a click as it turned. As this happened a small doorway opened in the chimney. He had to hunch over and almost crawl through, this is how small the doorway was. When he reached around and retrieved to key, the door began to slowly reseal itself behind him.

Jason quickly finished his whiskey and walked out of the tavern. The reason he did this is because while he was drinking his whiskey, he notice 2 men in dark suits wearing fedoras at the end of the bar. This was the type of place that you never see men in suits during the day, much less around midnight.

As Jason was driving down the road he was reasonably sure there was no one following him. Still, there was something about those 2 men at the tavern, that gave him a bad feeling. As he was driving up a hill he noticed a slow moving pickup truck hauling a trailer behind it. On the trailer there was a cub cadet riding mower, and various tools.

The truck was only moving about 20 miles per hour up the hill. Jason decided to pass the truck. He started passing the truck he heard a loud noise as the driver of the pickup floored the throttle. The back wheels of the pickup started smoking. As this happened Jason floored the pedal in his car. Because the pickup was pulling the trailer he wasn't going to be able to keep Jason from passing him. Jason's car was accelerating faster than the pickup truck. He was almost passed the pickup when suddenly the driver of the truck did a hard left and rammed his car. The force of the impact caused Jason's car to flip over the side of the road and tumble down about 20 feet into a ravine. The truck didn't even slowdown as it sped away.

Inside the chimney there was a steel ladder leading down. The hidden chimney door continued slowly resealing behind him as he made his way down the ladder.

The chimney ladder extended down about 200 total feet. About every 9 feet there was a triangular shaped ledge just off to the side. These ledges were there so those using the ladder could stop to rest, especially since anyone traveling through would most likely be carrying equipment and supplies.

When John Buck reached the ground level, he pulled out the map. According to the map he was in an underground network of artificially constructed caves and corridors. While some areas of the ground were bare dirt, other areas looked like carved bedrock. The walls were mostly solid carved rock. However, there were a few walls at various locations constructed of brick, some of steel plating etc. On the map there was a corridor that intersects the one he was in about 500 feet west. What really puzzled him is the pattern he noticed on the map. It looked like the standard map symbol for railroad tracks.

He started walking toward the intersection. Sure enough, there were railroad tracks running in the corridor. It was a railroad tunnel. John looked down and got a closer look at the tracks. From the appearance of the rust and track condition, he estimated that a train hadn't passed over these tracks for at least 10 years. After a momentary pause, he
xl

continued on his journey west another 200 feet. This course would take him almost directly beneath of where Dr Konavich was standing, smoking a cigar.

Suddenly he reached a dead end. According to the map, this end of the corridor is supposed to connect with a series of chambers or caverns. He was standing there thinking about the situation, when he noticed music. He approached the wall where the music was emanating from. There was a slot similar to the one in the chimney at the schoolhouse.

After inserting the key and turning it, a small 9 inch square panel slid open beside the key. Inside the recessed panel he could see a lighted keypad. However, John had no idea what the access code could be. He opened his bookbag to see if there was anything that could help him solve the problem.

He typed "*1885*" onto the keypad and pressed the enter button. The only thing that happened was the digits he previously enter flashed for about 5 seconds then disappeared. The screen was blank again.

"Idiot," John whispered to himself, "I was assuming it was a 4 digit combination like an ATM machine."

Realizing his error when he remembered that the display was 8 digits in length, he started punching numbers into the keypad.

"*1-8-8-5-1-9-6-2*"

This time as the numbers on the display were blinking, a doorway started to reveal itself. The music immediately increased in volume as the large 2 foot wide layered door slowly opened.

The inside walls and floor were of polished black granite, in stark contrast to the rough stone corridor on the other side of the entrance. The room was perfectly square with each side being 12 foot long, including the 12 foot high ceiling. It was like being inside a perfectly polished cube. There were only 3 things in this cube besides John Buck, a rug about 5 foot square in the center of the room, and 2 long sofas. The sofas were directly across from the rug opposite each other.

John walked over to the sofa on his right and carefully sat down at the end. The material was unlike anything he ever felt before. It was like a combination of the best leather, and a soft suede fabric, with a hint of the finest silk. The music he heard earlier appeared to be omnipresent. Somehow the sofa was transferring the sound-waves in greater complexity directly into his body. He was living the music. Sitting there with his eyes closed feeling the greatness of the symphony inside him he suddenly heard a voice had hadn't heard in years.

"You've arrived precisely within the hour predicted," Dr John Geiklan was saying, as the door on the other side of the room slowly resealed itself.

Dr Geiklan sat down in the opposite sofa across the rug from John Buck. At each of the sofas a 12 inch square column of granite began to slowly rise from the floor. They stopped about 2 feet higher than the arm of the sofas. While to top and 3 of the sides of each column were solid polished granite, the side facing each of them was not.

Dr Geiklan reached over to the column for the purpose of opening a small glass panel door. There was no handle that John could see on the glass panel facing him. He looked over to see Dr Geiklan press against the right side of the glass panel. There was a click, then the panel opened. Behind the glass in the column various items have been prepared. These were as follows: freshly brewed hot tea, a porcelain plate, and a cloth drawstring bag. On the plate were extra sharp white cheddar cheese, and green olives. The drawstring bag was infused with gourmet dehydrated meats.

They exchanged a few words of minor significance as they enjoyed the tea and food. Then there was a sound of movement from inside the columns. John looked inside and noticed a cigar, complete with a butane torch and ashtray. As they were puffing on the cigars Dr Geiklan spoke.

"Watch closely"

Then suddenly Dr Geiklan pressed the lit end of his cigar against the fabric of the sofa. When he pulled it back, there was no mark on the fabric.

"What type of fabric is that?" John was impressed.

Without saying a word, Dr Geiklan took his butane torch, turned it on full blast and held the flame against the sofa.

"Wow!"

"The fabric is something one of our best teams designed at the laboratory," Dr Geiklan said after taking a few more puffs from his cigar.

"It is bullet proof, acid proof, and can withstand all but the highest powered lasers. In fact we have to use a special high powered laser whenever we need to cut the fabric. This will be used to make the next bookbags issued to our members.

"When can I have a bookbag constructed of that fabric?"

"All in do time," Dr Geiklan said with the barest hint of a smile, and twinkle in his eye, "There is someone I have to introduce you to."

The hidden door at the side of the cube opposite the one John entered opened. They stepped out into a hallway and continued walking. The walls, ceiling and floor of the hallway were of polished copper. There was a rubber sheet about 2 inches thick on the floor for them to walk over. This was to prevent any possible conduction of electromagnetic radiation between the copper floor and the people traveling through the hallway. After walking about 25 feet, they came upon the end of the hallway. A camera was mounted above the large door. As they approached, the door autocratically opened for them. They walked through without slowing down.

The room they entered was about 25 feet wide and about 50 feet long, with a ceiling about 10 feet high. On one side, along the length of the room, were various pieces of equipment. John noticed some people carrying a heavy piece of machinery through the door at the far end of the room. They sat it down beside another similar looking machine. An other group of people were wearing blue lab coats, pants, and face masks walked over to the machines. They each carried a blue toolbox. The men in the blue lab coats started working on the new machinery. They appeared to be connecting the 2 machines together.

 In the middle of the room were a row of desks with leather chairs behind them. The desks were facing the center of the other long wall. In the center of the wall was some type of window about 20 feet wide. It appeared to be tinted and about 3 feet thick. John looked through the window.

The floor on the other side of the window was about 2 feet lower than the floor in the room they currently occupied. The ceiling of that room was about 4 feet higher. There was people wearing various colored lab coats working on the machinery. One of the machines had a huge silver coil about 5 feet in diameter total. It looked like a giant doughnut. There were 2 more giant donuts lined up. However, those other doughnuts appeared to be constructed of some type of dark brown material. Along the far wall were tanks of various liquids and gasses.

Dr Geiklan and John Buck walked over to an oval shaped conference table surrounded by leather chairs. This was an area of the room behind the row of desks, raised about 12 inches above the surrounding floor of the room. This made it easier for the people to watch the activities happening in the other room. John recognized one of the people sitting at the table, as the president of the local landfill division. Beside him was a man wearing a dark suit and a fedora hat.

"John Buck," Dr Geiklan began, "It is my pleasure to introduce you to Dr Konavich, the director of this laboratory."

"It is an honor to meet you," John said as he reached over to shake Dr Konavich's hand.

"No," Dr Konavich corrected him, "the honor is mine."

John and Dr Geiklan each sat down in chairs at the conference table. Dr Konavich began to speak.

"Mr Buck, first I have some unfortunate information to give you concerning your driver, Jason."

"What happened?" John showed no hint of shock or surprise, because he had mentally prepared himself for a series of worst case scenarios.

"It seems a demon was able to have enough influence over a driver of a pickup truck, causing him to ram Jason's car off the road. Fortunately, I was able to assign two of my best agents to watch out for Jason's safety, and should anything happen to him, they were to immediately take action on my behalf."

"What condition is he in?" John asked.

"He is currently recovering with a broken leg at our medical facility."

"And the driver?"

The three men at the table looked at each other, then looked at John. The landfill president touched the surface of the table in front of him. It lit up as the president started using the touchscreen interface. In the center of the table there was a glass crystal cube about 18 inches square. Inside the cube a holographic image of the landfill appeared. As the president manipulated his touchscreen panel, the image zoomed to a location of the landfill with a red pickup. They could see a real-time holographic motion of men with cutting torches scrapping the truck.

"As you can see the truck is currently being recycled. As for the driver, he is being held at an underground facility in Wyoming," Dr Konavich stated.

"Mr Buck," Dr Geiklan began speaking seriously about the situation, "when you first joined Order of the Bookbag about 3 years ago, I explained how demons are influencing and possessing key people in positions of authority. From the research we have been able to do, we know that powerful demonic entities do in fact hold most of the key positions in government."

"Now, the man driving the pickup truck was not possessed of a demon at first. Jason, your driver was the real target of the demonic forces of evil. However, as Jason was not an initiate into Order of the Bookbag, he did not have the

xlvii

full protection that comes with membership. Being a close associate did offer enough protection so that the demon could not influence Jason directly."

"Also, because these demons are of some extra dimensional entity, they seem to have the ability to see possible future events," Dr Geiklan continued, "It is likely that one of the demons foreseeing Jason eventually passing the pickup truck, was able to deduce that the path of least resistance was to influence and attempt to possess the driver of the pickup truck."

"Now," Dr Konavich began to speak, adding to the discussion, "While everyone including ourselves can feel or be affected by these inter-dimensional demonic entities, they can only have a sustained or continuous influence on a small percentage of the population."

"Are you saying that I have been influenced by demons too?" John Buck asked.

"Did you ever have an irrational thought, or be motivated to do something," Dr Konavich was saying, "that you later regretted, because there was no doubt as to the immorality of that action or motivation?"

Before John could answer, Dr Konavich continued, "Sometimes it may only be a split second, a momentary lapse of reason, before we catch ourselves, this comes from somewhere, because everything has a cause."

"While these small temporary indiscretions do cause some trouble to our world," Dr Geiklan was speaking now, "the true danger to the future of our world is from that percentage of people who are under constant influence from these demonic forces. Possessed, is simply defined as someone who is almost completely and continuously under the influence of a demon or demonic entity."

"The thing that makes these possessed people dangerous is that although they are a small percentage of the population, most of them seek positions of centralized authority and central control over property. Once they control these central positions of authority, they can expand and leverage the demonic influence over the rest of the population."

"Mr Stone," Dr Geiklan said as he turned to the president of the landfill division, "tell John Buck about the home office."

"Remember when you were first offered a full-time position at the landfill," Mr Stone began, "how I warned you about the drug test?"

"Yes"

"The drug prohibition laws and drug tests are demonically inspired. The whole purpose is to train and teach people to be treated like cattle. I am just the president of the local landfill who happens to be against these negative forces. The drug testing policy was ordered by the CEO of the Waste Corporation in Chicago. That is where the corporation headquarters is located."

"The CEO is possessed?" John asked.

xlix

"The larger a corporation or organization is, the more likely the top person in charge will be under demonic influence. This happens simply because the forces of evil will focus much more effort to acquire a position that has more centralized control of resources and authority. The parent corporation that owns this landfill happens to be the largest waste corporation in the USA."

"How were you able to hold onto the position of president of this landfill, if you oppose the demonic forces?"

"I had some help," Mr Stone spoke, "No one at the corporate home office knows about this underground facility. This is the reason Borace Mingela could not sell the rest of the land to the Waste corporation. Him and the organization he help to build, had to maintain control of this facility as leverage. Mr Mingela recognized the threat those demonic forces posed to humanity many years ago. The original contract he has with the Waste Corporation and landfill, gave him veto over the appointment of the local president in charge of this landfill."

As John sat there and took a drink of his tea, he was beginning to realize the true genius of Mr Mingela.

"As for the drug tests," Mr Stone continued, "the reason for the increasing level of drug testing throughout the waste corporation is to distract from the criminal activity of the CEO and key people on his executive management team."

1

"Criminal activity?" John did hear various rumors about the waste corporation be involve with organized crime, however, he considered such things in jest, at the time.

"The CEO along with some key people on the top executive team are embezzling money from the corporation. They are falsifying records and accounting. Whenever the top people in an organization are involved in that or similar activity they will almost immediately embark on a campaign of *'cracking down'* on the bottom half of the organizational chart."

"Meetings will be held, directives issued, memos sent out, rules will start to be tightened or restricted for the lower tier employees, responding to a non-issue. This is mainly to distract from the criminal activity happening at the top of the organizational chart."

John finished his tea.

"It looks like the criminal activity in the top executive team is starting to accelerate."

"How do you know this?" Dr Geiklan asked.

"Today I received a message that the CEO is ordering an increase in urine drug testing rates and in 3 months a mobile hair testing lab will be dispatched randomly to all Waste Corporation divisions. Those at the corporate headquarters in Chicago will be exempt from the drug testing. Everyone else will have to submit, and anyone who isn't as clean as a nun shall be fired on the spot."

As they sat around the conference table discussing events and such things, technicians in various colored lab coats were putting together and testing machinery. There was a team lead by an optical engineer responsible for aligning the massive doughnut shaped pieces in the large room. The doughnut shape devices create a powerful magnetic field. The reason those doughnut devices must be lined up perfectly has something to do with quantum coherence of energy shells surrounding the nucleus of atoms.

"....... that is why I shall be running for attorney general of Pennsylvania," Dr Geiklan was saying.

"John Buck," Dr Konavich had turned to him to ask a question, "Are you planning to run for office in the next election?"

"I narrowed it down to school board or town council," John answered, "I shall decide by the next meeting."

They discuss their political plans while the technicians were finishing testing out the machinery. One key thing they had decided was that they were not going to run as republicans or democrats. It was decided they were forming a new political party. This party was founded for the purpose of repelling the inter-dimensional demonic problem. Since the demons could only possess a small percentage of the population, the solution was quite simple. Convince enough of the good people to run for political office and vote. If the people knew the true power they really had, they could sweep aside those small percentage of demon infested people like dust.

For about 2 seconds there was a loud buzzing noise, like an alarm. When this happened Dr Konavich stood up.

"Excuse me gentlemen, I believe we are almost ready."

Dr Konavich walked over to a man wearing a red lab coat, and they spoke for about 30 seconds. Then Dr Konavich returned to the conference table.

"Unfortunately at this time, we don't even have enough people running for office to take over the government, even if they all won," Dr Geiklan was saying in frustration, "but suppose we did, and did take over, then what?"

"That would not solve the problem of the inter-dimensional demonic invasion," John answered.

"Precisely," Dr Geiklan was almost shouting, "in fact there is a very high probability that when we start having political success, there will be a massive desperate focus of demonic energy across the dimensional membrane."

"The equipment in this facility was designed to test a theory about the membrane, and find a way to stop this invasion," Dr Konavich was saying.

"You are planning to save the world from a landfill?" John asked.

"This is the perfect location for a variety of reasons," Mr Stone began to speak, "however, the most important reason is, our new waste to energy plant we just finished at the corner of the landfill. Remember the power generating

liii

capacity I spoke about at the town council when the energy plant was approved?"

"Yes."

"Obviously I could not tell them the actual capacity of our advanced waste to energy technology," Mr Stone was saying, "that would put us in jeopardy of being discovered."

"I can imagine it would take a massive amount of electricity to power this underground base," John was pondering aloud.

"When we are fully operational," Dr Konavich was speaking, "it will take approximately 1 million times the publicly stated electric generating capacity, to power this facility."

"The actual generating capacity of our waste to energy system is almost 2 million times what I told the town council," Mr Stone said, with a hint of a smile. Then he leaned back in his chair and lit a cigar.

Presently there were technicians taking seats at the desks that were lined up facing the window into the other room. At the same time display panels lit up in front of each of the men sitting around the conference table. The display in front of John Buck had some information about a countdown, along with some video feeds from cameras. While John Buck and Mr Stone were just watching their displays, Dr Konavich and Dr Geiklan hands were rapidly moving over their touchscreen interfaces. As they were working they would periodically glance up at the crystal cube in the center of the table.

Inside the cube the holographic display started to display different images. While John did recognize some of the images, he soon realized there was something bizarre about some of them. It was showing different places around the world. Each for about 2 or 3 seconds then the hologram would suddenly change to another seemingly random image.

As this was happening the liquid nitrogen was being pumped through tubes from the tanks to the large doughnut shaped devices. Some frost was appearing on the cryogenic tubing. What appeared to be smoke emanating from the doughnut devices was really evaporating liquid nitrogen reacting with the surrounding air. A slow deep hum could be heard and felt throughout the facility. This hum was steadily increasing in pitch and speed.

Then there was a change in the holograms displaying through the crystal cube. While the holograms were still images at first, now they were beginning to show action. Instead of a still image of a bird, it the bird's wings would be flapping as it moved through the air.

When John Buck looked down to the display in front of him he saw there was 2 minutes left in the countdown.

1:59

Each scene would have more detail and motion as they got closer to the end of the countdown. There would be a dog walking. Then people sitting at a table playing cards in a lv smoke filled room. Then from the vantage point of an airplane or helicopter, he would see a city skyline, or a rural area. One of the holograms showed a couple in a bed having sex. Then suddenly there was a scene of a baby crying filling the whole cube.

1:17

"What the hell?"

"What did you see?" Dr Konavich said as he looked up from his display.

"I just saw a jet crash into one of the world trade center towers in New York City," Mr Stone said in shock.

1:10

John Buck and Mr Stone watched the cube as Dr Konavich and Dr Geiklan continued working.

1:07

"MARTHA!" Mr Stone cried out. He had a look of pain, anguish, and shock on his face.

What Mr Stone saw was 2 different holograms. The first was of him married to Martha with 3 children the youngest being about 7 years old. The 2nd hologram was of an older Martha and Mr Stone, as grandparents. But Martha died when she was 24 years old in a plane crash. The were briefly lovers in high school with then they broke up and went there separate ways.

Over the years Mr Stone always wondered what would have happened if things did work out between them. At age 24 she married a fellow she met at her work. They were flying to their honeymoon in Hawaii when the plane they were on crashed into the ocean.

1:00

The holograms that were being displayed in the cube were from parallel universes. They were opening up a window into these places. Some were almost identical to the one they were in, some were slightly different, some were vastly different. This technology was based on a new variation of M theory that Dr Konavich and Dr Geiklan simultaneously deduced.

This new M theory, they call the 6 dimensional symmetry. Up until that point there was the problem of superimposition of the quantum state conflicting with only having 1 dimension of space-time. There was the conventional 3 spacial dimensions that the most basic geometry student knows about. The other physicists who previously worked on M Theory were correct that the fabric of the universe was a membrane and that all matter atoms, electrons, were actually strings woven into the fabric of the membrane. There was no such thing as empty space, the apparent affect of forces from a distance like gravity and electromagnetism were just folds and tensions in the fabric of this membrane. However, they made one basic flawed assumption. In order to make their theory fit, they kept on adding more spatial dimensions, while keeping the time dimension at just 1. So by the time Dr Konavich and Dr Geiklan solved the problem, the leading M Theorist of the day were claiming membranes with 10 or even 11 dimensions, all save 1 were simply extra junk spacial dimension, staying with a single dimension of time.

The solution was simple, spatial geometry should have symmetry with time itself. And so, we end up with a membrane of 6 total dimensions, 3 geometric, and 3 of time.

0:45

Holograms continued to speed up. There was a scene of a man wearing a military uniform, giving orders to others in a war.

Then more random scenes. Then what appeared to be the same man much younger, possibly a teenager in a car. The car was being struck by bullets. There was another young man beside him in the car who appeared to have something wrong with one of his eyes. Then more random holograms.

0:15

When the countdown was down to 15 seconds the holograms were changing so fast, that the cube became a blur. The acceleration of the holograms continued at such a scale that would approach infinity as the countdown reached zero.

lviii

0:05

The crystal cube was a flashing rainbow of colors.

0:03

The flashing rainbow of colors were merging together toward white.

0:02

At this point the cube was becoming a solid white glow and getting brighter.

0:01

At this point there was a noticeable glow that was getting brighter from the other room. This was emanating from the center of the doughnut devices.

At the zero mark there would only be a 1 second window where the device could open a gateway into a parallel universe. The computer was programmed with a triple activation fail-safe interlock.

0:00

At this point the cube was such a bright white glow that no one in the room could look directly at it. The men who sat at the table had closed their eyes. Dr Konavich and Dr Geiklan were prepared for this moment. Even with their eyes closed they placed their hands palm facing the touchscreen interface. The computer recognized not just the pattern on the skin, but also the bone structure and blood vessel patterns. A third man in another room unaffected by the glow from the cube was watching by closed circuit video. The third man had to place his hand down on his touchscreen interface at the same time during the window as the other 2 men.

The moment the three men activated the gateway a number of things happened simultaneously. The high pitched sound of the device stopped and there was almost total silence. The glow from the doughnuts disappeared. The crystal cube stopped glowing white and inside the cube there was a fading still hologram. The hologram took a few seconds to fade as the men sat there in shock.

"What the hell is that?" John asked.

Then Mr Stone burst out laughing. Soon all 4 men at the conference table were laughing. The cube was predicted to stop showing a hologram of a specific event in a parallel universe. This was to be a point across the multidimensional membrane as close to the gateway as possible. However, the event in the cube could be anywhere from fractions of a second to months from the actual gateway point in space-time.

The fading hologram was both of a man's buttocks over a cardboard box and of a dark brown feces in high-definition 3d frozen in a moment in time as it was falling between the buttocks and the bottom of the box. That was the only thing visible. After a few seconds the hologram faded out from the outside of the cube to the center. This had the added effect because the feces was in the center of the cube, it was the last to disappear. Then the cube was transparent and empty.

The gateway itself was opened in a spherical area about 18 inches in diameter. This was directly in front of the doughnut devices. At the table they played back the video recorded by the high-speed cameras of the gateway event. There was a pinpoint of light that rapidly expanded to an 18 inch glowing sphere. Then the glow collapsed down to a rectangular box shape. The box itself was momentarily glowing then the glow faded as it fell to the floor.

Men in fully contained NBC suits entered the airlock. After waiting the 15 minutes for the airlock to cycle the door to the gateway chamber opened. They walked over to the box and looked it over. There was a light fog or vapor rolling off the surface. On the floor were shards of ice that were already beginning to melt. The box itself seemed to be covered with a thin layer of ice and frost. The men were scanning the box and surrounding area with hand held radiation meters. There was also a spectrographic analyzer.

The men at the table were watching all this on their display panels when the voice of one of the men could be heard from the speakers mounted above the table. With gloved hands one of them had just picked up the box and brushed off the frost on the top surface. There appeared to be a delivery address along with a date stamped on the outside of the box.

"Dr Konavich," the voice from the speakers was saying, "are you seeing this?"

"Yes"

"Watch the monitor while I hold the box up to the camera."

There was close to 75 people total at various locations throughout the facility, watching the camera feed on monitors. From one of the desks at the far end of the room could be heard the sound of a coffee mug shattering as it hit the floor. From another location someone gasped for air in shock. At the conference table the 3 men were momentarily frozen as they saw what was on the outside of the box.

"How could this happen?" John asked.

Dr Geiklan leaned back in his chair as the shock was disappearing from his face. He reached into an inside pocket and pulled out 3 items. A cigar cutter, a cigar, and a butane torch. They sat there for a few moments watching the display. Then Dr Konavich started working his touchscreen panel. He was doing calculations and replaying video feeds.

On the outside of the box was a name, *John Konavich.* There was a barcode tracking label, with a shipped by date of *December 18, 2012.*

"I believe it may be from a parallel universe of about 15 years future," Dr Geiklan was saying.

"This was not just a simple lateral shift of energy," Dr Konavich added.

"A lateral shift?" John asked.

"Today's date is November 19, 1996," Dr Konavich was explaining, "If this was a simple lateral shift then the latest shipped by date that could be on the label is November 19, 1996. Of course it would be a November 19, in a parallel universe along one of the other time dimensions. Since this box has a shipped date in 2012, we know that it is along more than one axis in the 3 time dimensional matrix.

"Do we have authorization to open the box?" a voice could be heard from every speaker in the facility.

"I hereby grant authorization," Dr Geiklan said as he placed his hand down on his touchscreen panel.

"I hereby grant authorization," Dr Konavich said and also placed his hand down on his panel.

"I concur," Mr Stone simply said.

One by one people in the facility repeated the phrase *I concur* when the panel in front of them started blinking. Finally the panel in front of John started blinking.

"John?" Dr Geiklan asked.

"I concur," John said when he realized it was his turn.

As soon as John gave approval an alarm sounded for 2 seconds, followed by a computer recording of a warning.

The technicians had a special toolbox. Inside the toolbox there was all types of special tools for manipulation objects. They placed the box in a cabinet with 2 thick glass walls for them to observe it while they prepared the tools.
Three cameras were pointed at the box. Just below each glass window was a set of hand insertion tubes. They placed the tools to be used into a draw and slide the draw into the cabinet. Then they reached into the tubes and grabbed the tools.

Each technician had a pair of gripper manipulator devices. They noticed the box was taped shut. One of the technicians pressed a button and a razor blade extended out of his device. As the other technician held the box, he carefully began to slide the blade across one of the box seams, slicing the tape. As soon as the blade was past the last bit of tape the one side of the box pushed out about 1 quarter inch. This was nothing more than the releasing of the tension that the box had from the tape on it. Nevertheless, there was a sudden sound of someone gasping for air then the breathing was normal again.

A few people at various locations in the facility sighed in relief at this point. However, it wasn't over.

One technician looked across at the other, when he saw the sweat dripping off his coworker's face, he realized he was also sweating.

"Ready?"

"Let's do this."

They slowly opened the box. It was only their intensive training spent in simulators that stopped them from jumping or having a serious reaction.

Shouts and loud talking could be heard throughout the facility. For some strange reason Mr Stone was taking a sip of coffee when he saw the inside of the box. Coffee was instantly propelled out of his mouth onto the conference table in front of him.

At this point Dr Konavich worked the panel in front of him for a few seconds. This caused a column to descend from the ceiling above to the table. Under the column a robotic cleaning device took care of the coffee mess. On the side of the column was a tray holding glasses with ice in them, along side a large bottle of scotch.

"Gentlemen," Dr Konavich began, "I don't know about the rest of you, but after that, I need a drink."

"What about the contents of the box?" Mr Stone asked.

"The feces shall be tested at the laboratory," Dr Konavich said.

"Dr Konavich," John asked, "Do you have a relative named John Konavich?"

"I once had an older brother named John Konavich. After he graduated high school he went into the seminary to train for the priesthood. He was about to be ordained when he was under continued assault by demons. Eventually he was committed to a mental institution. It was during my conversations with him at the mental institution that I started to formulate my theory about the inter-dimensional demonic entities."

"We originally set the machine to open a gateway at a random coordinate laterally close to our own time-frame," Dr Geiklan was saying, "Looking at the replays of the holograms and what came through the gateway, it appears that the gateway coordinates are somehow affected by the people involved in running the machine itself."

"We may have to suspend gateway operations for awhile so we can crunch the data"

They spoke for a time at the table then it was time to adjourn the meeting.

"It it settled we meet at the Bull Dog tavern in one month to recruit candidates for next year's election," Dr Geiklan said.

For the next few months they worked to find and recruit candidates to run for office among other things.

Chapter 5

Evidence of the Demonic Power

As the CEO of the Waste corporation accelerated his self dealing, more directives were issued. Drug tests were continuously expanded. There was talk of requiring credit checks for new job applicants. Of course such things would not be asked of any potential new member of the executive team. Such things are only for the little people. Eventually one day John Buck was warned that the directive was issued to start hair testing for drugs. There must be some serious criminal activity at the corporate office. Most likely involving drug fueled orgies with prostitutes.

Any basic psychology student knows of a thing called *projection*.

This is where the individual subconsciously projects their own negativity or self-guilt onto others. One example of projection most people know about is infidelity in a committed monogamous relationship. One person will be unfaithful in the relationship and then project (i. e. accuse and/or look for evidence that their partner has been unfaithful) that guilt onto someone else. They do this to justify their own lack of integrity.

Obviously a similar thing was happening at the Waste Corporation. There were key people in the executive office who were addicted to drugs, or just like to use drugs like weed that were currently politically unpopular in the USA at the time. Most likely they were into hard drugs like cocaine and/or methamphetamine, as someone who is only an occasional user of pot is less likely to consider their lifestyle choice a character defect.

Put another way, most theft in big business is committed by those in a management position. That is to say while there is certainly theft and other forms of moral wrongdoing being perpetrated by those at the bottom of an organizational chart (entry level, hourly employees etc.), Using moral integrity as a yardstick, it is clear that the fish rots from the head.

Then one day John Buck was working sorting trash in one of the intake buildings.

"Hey, John Buck," the department shift lead was shouting because of the noisy machinery, "you need to go to the office, the mobile drug test lab is here."

Even with the shift lead shouting, he could barely understand what was said. He knew he had to go to the office and started walked in that direction. As he did this, there was one thought on his mind.

Did he say, "drug test lab?"

Beside the office was the mobile drug test lab.

"They are waiting for you over there John," the manager was standing there outside, pointing at the lab.

It looked like a converted RV or bus. Inside were some rooms with technicians to perform the test. He looked around and saw two other employees of his department getting a small clump of hair cut from their head.

As they cut a clump of hair from his head, John swore to himself this was the last time he would endure such humiliation. He passed a urine test when he was first hired, as all new employees had to pass one before their first day. Now that wasn't good enough. Now it was cutting of his hair so it could be analyzed by a laboratory. One thing is clear from history, appeasing a bully or some CEO executive who likes to push people around only emboldens them. If they would settle for this, there was no limit. What was next? Blood tests, DNA profiles, proctology Exams?

As John returned to work he noticed the shift lead approach others in his department. He couldn't hear what was said, just him pointing in the direction of the mobile drug test lab. Then they would walk over to have hairs cut from their heads. This was odd, because it was written that the official drug test policy was random drug tests for current employees.

How can it be random if they are testing everyone on the same day?

There was talk about a number people who worked at the landfill division getting fired for failing the hair test. These were outstanding professional people who passed every urine test they ever took previously. There were rumors that the test was inaccurate.

Soon after John gave notice of resignation to the manager.

Years later an investigation was conducted by a private detective. There was evidence of bribery and self dealing involving a former executive of the Waste corporation who is a major shareholder of the company that owns the laboratory conducting the hair drug tests. There was an obvious conflict of interest in addition to possible insider trading. However, the players involved were playing by a different set of rules. That is to say, it is easier to get away with something clearly illegal when one has plenty of wealth. This is not necessarily to hire defense attorneys to defend in court. For the mere fact that one is independently wealthy is usually enough to prevent such things from making it to a courtroom in the first place. Either through bribery or other kinds of payoffs.

Hence it is true that most rules are for those at the bottom of the social-economic strata. It is much easier to push someone around who is close to broke, a person who's income can barely buy them the basic necessities. One thing I do know is, that pushing people around is something those who control the fortune 500 corporations love to do. That will be addressed later. If not in this book, then another. For now let us return to the adventures of John Buck across the infinite.

"I'll have a draft beer," John said to the bartender. He had just entered the Bull Dog tavern and was sitting at the end of the bar.

There they discussed politics and other such things.

"We have a window of time to collect enough signatures to put our people on the ballot for the election in November," Woody Smith was saying.

And so the job of collecting signatures was divided among the members of the party. Candidates would leave the meeting with petitions for office.

This was John Buck's first year of collecting signatures. He started by walking around the neighborhood knocking on doors.

"Hello, my name is John Buck," He would say, "I am collecting signatures to put my name on the ballot for town council."

Some people would sign his petition some would not. One thing he noticed was a general difference in attitudes and respect between the women and men he spoke to. The men seemed for the most part to be more respectful. There was one man he met who clearly showed contempt for John and his politics. That man turned out to be someone who profited from tyranny and fascism. He was an attorney on the government payroll, receiving tax dollars. This was something John could understand, even if it was evil. The attitude of the women he did not understand.

Sometimes he would knock on a door and a woman would answer the door who appeared to be in her twenties and with some inherent beauty. Sometimes such women would sign the petition, sometimes not. A few of them acted in such a way that, John walked away in shock and bewilderment.

"Hello, my name is John Buck. I am collecting signatures to put my name on the ballot for town council."

At this point the reaction was such that a deaf man watching from a distance might think that John Had just said, "Yo Babe, show me your tits."

Going out to meetings campaigning door to door, taught John about the nature of the average American. He felt in his soul that there was something wrong with the way people are. It was like most people were herd animals who never had an original thought in their life.

Meanwhile John had been working on a campaign to send a member of his new political party to congress. He was a smart man of integrity who would make a fine representative in congress.

"You going to be at the election celebration tonight?" Jason asked John.

"I have to be at the polls when the close, so I can get the final vote results. Afterward, I'll stop in at the party."

John walked into the bar where the victory celebration was being held. Some people were talking, as others were watching the big screen television. At one corner the candidate for congress was sitting beside a shady looking character, who turned out to be a reporter for the local newspaper.

"You should run as a republican instead of wasting time running under the banner of this minor fringe party," Mark was saving dripping with venom.

"My whole reason for running is to stand for principle," Mr Stone was saying, "besides, since I would most likely not get the republican nomination, then there would be no one on the ballot in November defending liberty."

They spoke for a few minutes then the shady reporter walked out of the bar.

John sat there watching the numbers roll in from the races across the nation. Mr Stone received less than 4 percent of the vote for congress. Most of the other candidates on the party ticket received about the same percentage of the vote. How could this happen? Why would someone who wanted to reduce the tyranny of the government, get such few votes?

John was thinking about how the Jews in Germany must have felt when the Nazi where winning elections.

Just when things were at a low point, suddenly loud cheers could be heard around the bar.

"Jesse Ventura won the Governor of Minnesota," a woman was shouting across the bar.

While Mr Ventura was not a member of the same political party as John Buck, he spoke of freedom and reducing the size of the government bureaucracy. There was a record percentage of people who showed up to vote in Minnesota. Last count was showing over 70 percent of the population eligible to vote, actually went to the polls. Most elections in a non-presidential election year have less than a 50 percent turnout. Since about 25 percent of the population benefits directly from government, (they are a bureaucrat, police, etc) a turnout of less than 50 to 60 percent will guarantee a steady growth of the size of government and tyranny. Those in the 25 percent who work for the government in some capacity have over a 90 percent turnout rate for elections, verses less than 30 percent on average of those in the productive areas of the economy.

The solution was simple, convince the other 50 to 60 percent of the population to vote. If they knew the power they held, they would sweep aside this tyranny effortlessly.

Chapter 6

A New Journey

"It looks like things are getting worse in the executive suite of the Waste Corporation," Mr Stone was saying.

"Also, it looks like Mr Mingela's health is starting to fade," Dr Konavich was saying, "we must start preparing for a relocation of our operations."

"We'll need to find another secure location to set up operations," Dr Geiklan added.

"I am planning a trip out west across the USA and possibly Canada," John Buck was saying.

They spoke for about an hour.

".......that is why you will need arctic gear," Dr Konavich was saying.

They spoke for a few more minutes then the meeting was adjourned. In the parking lot after the meeting he spoke with a few of his close associates who he trusted with his like. Only a handful of people knew his true destination or mission. Those he spoke with in the parking lot were sworn to secrecy.

"When I pull out of this parking lot," John began, "I'll shall be on my journey."

"You are already packed up?" Jason asked as he walked over to John's car.

"Yes, I am not playing games."

"Looks like your rear window has some condensation on it."

"That's OK," John Buck replied loudly and almost laughing, as he prepared to drive away, "I am going forward NOT backward."

Chapter 7

Traveling Across a Continent

Earth Summer 1999 AD

Gasoline had dipped below 1 dollar a gallon for the first time in years. John drove for almost 24 hours that first day, only stopping to refill the gas tank. He finally pulled into a parking lot of a rest-stop and promptly fell asleep in his car.

The 2nd day he saw massive numbers of people on motorcycles as he entered South Dakota. Later he discovered this is a motorcycle rally called Sturgis. John saw many things in South Dakota that day, prairie dogs, badlands, an old ghost town. Near the late afternoon he reached the western border of South Dakota. When he saw the casino he decided to investigate.

As he walked down the hall toward the casino rooms he saw velvet ropes with people dressed in fancy uniforms standing by.

"Welcome to the casino," said the watchdog, "may I see your identification."

There wasn't much activity in the casino. John looked around at the rows of slot machines. The reason for doing this is to see if people are winning. In this case a bell starts ringing continuously when a slot machine is paying out winnings. The lower the "crowd : bell ringing" ratio, the better. Example; A casino with hardly any people in it, and constant bell ringing from people winning, is great. At the other end of the scale, you have a casino packed with a massive crowd of people gambling, and almost no bell ringing, very bad. The casino John walked into that day was closer to the first example.

John sat down at a slot machine and started playing. It was only a few minutes until he won about 75 dollars. Immediately after being up over 75 dollars he moved on to another slot machine. There he hit another 130 dollars within 10 minutes. Shortly after winning a nice amount on 2 machines, he walked out of the casino with the bucket filled with quarters. He didn't even stop to cash them in. As he walked out of the casino carrying the bucket, he felt like a god.

He crossed the Wyoming border just after dusk. As it got dark he started noticing strange streaks of light flashing in the sky. Sometimes the brightest ones would have a green glow to them. It turned out to be a great meteor shower. He pulled his car off the side of the highway to get some sleep. As he watched the meteor shower he thought of what may exist out there beyond the Earth.

Are there other people on other planets?

After dreaming of meteors, he woke up to sunlit rocky mountains to his west.

John Buck spent most of the day driving in Wyoming and into Montana. Then around noon he approached the high rocky mountains. At the bottom of the mountains a sign was posted along the road.

Warning: Check brakes, and mount chains on your tires if the road conditions are bad.

Drivers of 18 wheelers were checking their rigs along the side of the road, before proceeding. Sometimes a column of camouflage Humvees with various support vehicles would pass through. John began the journey up the mountain.

He continuously drove his car up the semi steep highway along the side of the mountain range. Suddenly the overheating engine light started glowing bright red. He pulled his car over along the side of the highway shut the engine off to let it cool down. After a time when he thought the engine was sufficiently cool enough to proceed he resumed his journey. After driving for another 20 minutes he saw a big sign along the highway stating he was now crossing the continental divide in the rocky mountains.

Suddenly the engine overheat flashed on the dashboard. John Buck Pulled over along the side of the highway right near the crest of the mountain. He shut the engine off, a few seconds later there was an explosion under the hood of the car and a big cloud of smoke rolled out. After waiting to make sure the car was not on fire, he leaned his seat back and went to sleep.

Chapter 8

Discovering the Cave

Shane and his wife are what some people may apply the label of hippie. They liked to go exploring wilderness areas, caves and such things. After spending most of the morning exploring a thickly forested area along a side of a mountain they discovered something.

"Those trees seem to be much older than the rest around here," Shane said as he started walking toward a group of trees that seemed out of place from the rest of the forest.

There was definitely something strange about that group of trees. They walked closer and then notice the entrance of a cave, close to the center of the ancient trees. While it did look like a natural cave, it also had an artificial look to it. Shane walked about 2 or three feet in front of his wife, with his hand on the revolver he had in his conceal holster ready in case some bear or other animal came running out of the cave to attack them.

Jennifer noticed Shane appeared to walk faster and faster as he approached the entrance. However there was something bizarre in the way he was walking. Then she realized it was like one of the old black and white films where everything is twice as fast. Shane was almost to the entrance of the cave when he suddenly looked back to see instead of being only 2 or 3 feet behind him, she was now about 30 feet behind. She appeared to be moving in slow motion. Shane stood there in awe of what he was seeing. He watched as his wife walk toward him. Her speed of movement increased until she was moving at the normal speed about 2 feet from Shane.

"What the hell?" they both simultaneously said at once. Then they heard the sound of a small explosion coming from the direction of the highway. It rumbled on for many minutes. As they stood there they notice the sounds of the forest were different. It was of a slower speed. They could hear the sounds of the cars from the highway clearer there than they could before they entered the strange tree location. They sounded like they were going about 10 miles per hour or even slower.

They started walking away from the area back toward the highway to see if there was some sort of accident. Perhaps someone needed their help.

"Look at that bird," Jennifer said to Shane.

Shane looked up to see a bird in the sky appeared to be flying in slow motion. As they walked away from the cave, the speed of the bird increased until it was at normal flying speed. After they were about 100 feet from the strange trees, they could no longer hear the traffic on the highway again. They spent a few hours walking the 5 miles back to the highway.

John Buck woke up after sleeping for about two hours. He opened the hood of his car to see the damage from the explosion. He noticed that one of the radiator hoses exploded. That was good news in that all he had to do is get a new radiator hose and refill the coolant. The bad news, he is out on the continental divide almost an hour from the nearest town.   He started walking along the side of the highway. About a half hour later a green Volkswagen stopped.

"You look like you need a ride," the driver of the car said.

"Yes, my radiator hose exploded in my car back the road," John replied.

As John sat down on the back seat, he felt a great relief to know he would not have to walk all the way into town.

"My name is Shane, and this is my wife Jennifer," Shane stated as they started driving away.

"My name is John," John said, "Thanks for stopping to offer me this ride into town."

During the drive to town Shane and Jennifer told John about how they happened to be in the area hiking. They did not mention the cave or the strange event that happened earlier. John told them he was traveling across North American from the east coast to Alaska.

When to arrived at the town and John started to pull cash out of his pocket to pay for the radiator hose and coolant, Shane told John he would pay for it. Shane waited back at John's car until he finished repairs and had it running again.

After John drove away Shane and his wife started making plans for exploring that strange cave they discovered earlier in the day. They would need to purchase a few more specialized supplies before they go back and explore it properly. They also made note to bring the dog next time. Perhaps the dog would notice anything unusual before they did. The dog could serve as an early warning. They also discussed the possibility that the special mushrooms may have affected them, and there was not really anything unusual about that area.

A few days later Shane and his wife were hiking toward the cave. They each had backpacks with supplies. Their dog was with them. This time they decided they would be sure to walk side by side. As they approached the area, they immediately started noticing the bizarre time warp affects. It was the dog they noticed first. The dog started barking and would run ahead of them. They noticed the speed of the dog would go into fast forward as he put distance between himself and his caretakers. However, as the dog would run back toward them he would suddenly return to normal speed. Then they saw the dog run in circle behind them. Suddenly the dog was running in slow motion, then returned to normal as he would get back closer to Shane and Jennifer.

Shane strapped on a special led light to his hat. Jennifer decided to carry a flashlight in her hand. They entered the cave.
The cave passage near the entrance was only about 3 or 4 feet wide and about 8 to 10 feet high. This passage slowly widened for about 30 feet then they entered a large cavern about 100 feet in diameter and with about a 20 to 30 foot at the highest point. They also notice that the cave became less natural and more artificial as they progressed into the larger cavern.

"Do you see that?" Jennifer said looking at the walls.

"Looks like symbols and some language I can't recognize," Shane was saying.

They walked across the cavern until they reached the wall. It appeared to be an almost perfectly smooth polished stone, with the exception of the symbols and writing carved into it. Along the wall there were two pillars of the same polished stone like material about 3 feet high connected to it. Then they noticed there were two pillars along each of other walls in the great cavern. Each set of pillars were about 22 feet apart. They could barely hear a steady low humming sound. On the top of the pillar they stood beside they noticed the same language and 2 hand prints carved side by side.

Shane placed his right hand against the carving of a right hand. Then he placed his left hand down against the other carving beside it. As soon as he did this he felt an energy almost like touching an electric wire except without the pain. About 2 feet in front of his face a small blue dot appeared. The blue dot immediately expanded into a hologram of the Earth.

Jennifer looked at Shane and saw that he froze like a statue the moment both hands were touching the top of the pillar.

"Shane," she spoke loudly, "are you alright?"

Shane slowly opened his mouth and replied, "yes."

He appeared to be staring at nothing in particular. He realized he is connected to some type of supercomputer that is communicating directly with his mind through the nerve fibers in his hands. The holograms he saw are only in his own mind. With his thoughts he could manipulate the holograms in front of his face. He saw a flashing red dot on the Earth hologram marking the place in Montana where the entrance to the cave is located. Then he saw other dots briefly light up as he searched other areas of North America. After a time, he removed his hands from the pillar.

"Your turn," he said to Jennifer.

When she put her hands down she suddenly took a deep breath as her eyes got big with awe. As she was communicating with the device, Shane walked over to the other pillar facing the same wall. He placed his hands down on the carvings. Now each of them had a hologram of the Earth along with other data.

This is so cool

It is some super advanced transportation system.

They were telepathically link through the device. They could communicate much faster than they could just talking.

They learned how this room is a junction point that connects tunnels with other points on the continent of North America. Those tunnels were once part of a larger transportation network, but larger parts of it were lost either by natural disaster, or war. They could not find out exactly what happened because the database was limited to the operation of the transportation system. However, they could tell this computer once had a connection to a library of historical records, that was severed some unknown time in the past.

Each of the 3 walls in the chamber led to a different transportation tunnel. According to the database hologram, one led to the Mt Shasta area, another near the Kansas city area of the mid-west. The wall they were facing was the end of a tunnel leading to a place in Alaska

After a few minutes of being connected to the device, the wall between their pillars started to have a green shimmer to it. Then it slowly faded away until it was almost totally transparent. As this happened they removed their hands from the pillars and with the dog beside them they walked through the transparent shimmering wall. About 22 seconds after they entered and were walking down the tunnel, the wall slowly became solid again. The shimmering stopped, and the great cavern was empty again.

Chapter 9

Alaska

John Buck was driving in Canada and did not want to waste money on lodging. He found a nice out of the way place to pull over along the Alaska highway in Northern Canada. He looked up a saw the great northern lights. They were directly overhead in the highest point of the sky, not some distant glow near the horizon. The next day John stopped to fill up his gas tank as well as pick up a bite to eat.

"Looks like Elizabeth is also the queen of Canada," John remarked, as he handed over some Canadian currency to pay for his goods.

"What are you talking about?" the ignorant Canadian replied.

"You have Elizabeth on your Canadian currency," John stated with authority.

The ignorant Canadian who never had an original thought in his life said, "Canada does not have a queen, we are independent."

"Then why does your currency have a queen on all of it?" John asked.

The ignorant Canadian continued to attempt to argue, spouting gibberish. John walked away because he knew it was a waste of time to argue with the fool.

Eventually one fine afternoon John crossed the border into Alaska. It would be almost another 2 days before he arrived at his destination to meet with his contact in Anchorage.

"My Name is Al Johnson," he introduced himself and another key member of the underground, "this is James Smith."

In a nondescript out of the way neighborhood on the west side of Anchorage, Alaska three men were meeting in the downstairs apartment of a two unit building owned by one of the leaders of the resistance. That leader's name is Leon. It is Leon who rented the downstairs apartment to other members of the resistance. He didn't ask many questions, he gave leeway to tenants if the rent was late. One thing about being in a freedom resistance movement is the lack of funds. Hence, one reason why rent was sometimes late and Leon understood this. His generosity was one of his many contributions to the resistance. Meanwhile downstairs the plan was discussed.

"Here is what we have planned for the next few months," Al spoke with the authority of someone who spent many years in politics.

At 23 years old, John was relatively new to politics. However, Al Johnson was in his 40's and James Smith was in his mid 30's. Both of these men left their private careers behind to dedicate their lives full time to fighting against the tyranny that was devouring the world. They knew what was at stake in the future. They dreamed of a world that was free from coercive taxes, prison industrial complexes, and central banks robbing the laboring classes of their earnings. It is a dream so important to them that they have slept in cars, on couches in people's living rooms, worked in the underground scrounging for any funding they could get to fight for the world they want to achieve.

"We are currently collecting signatures to put 2 initiatives on the ballot for next years November election," Al continued, "one is a property tax cap, and the other is to take away all of Alaska's court's jurisdiction to prosecute hemp or cannabis."

"There is also the Alaska state fair in a few weeks," James said.

Al, James, and John talked for almost an hour. In a few days John would be working with James helping to collect signatures for the balloting proposals.

John Buck spent a few days exploring the local town. After working a few old laboring jobs, he got a job as a pizza delivery driver.

"Bad news John," Fred said as he handed John the print out of his next deliver, "upper-class neighborhood."

It was only his first week delivering pizzas and John received respectable tips. However, he had only been delivering to working class neighborhoods his first few days.

"How can that be bad news?'" John asked. He made the mistake of thinking logically and ethically, still young he was naive about the nature of people.

"Wealthier people barely tip, if at all," Fred replied.

John didn't believe it until he started delivering to upper-class neighborhoods. He was stunned at the hypocrisy the financially independent people had regarding property rights. One time he was making a delivery to an upper middle class house (2 football Fields could fit into the front yards alone of the average house between the street and the front door) and he stopped his car along the street to look around. Almost immediately he heard yelling from a distance. He looked over to see a spoil brat female standing at her open front door yelling at him.

"Stop parking in my yard!"

John had not parked in her yard. His car was stopped along the street and there was about 2 football Bucks distance between the edge of the road, his car and her front door. He continued delivering pizzas for about another 2 weeks before encountering another rude spoiled brat female when he quit.

c

"Deja vu," Karen said.

"What did you say?" John replied to her as he turned in her direction.

"Deja vu," She said, "I remember living this before."

"Oh," John said, "I think I had that experience a few times in my life before, they seem to last only a few seconds, like a dream I can't remember."

Karen only nodded her head with a small hint of a smile as John talked.

"That was the best sex I ever had," Karen said, as she was looking up at the ceiling above the bed, "even better than the dream."

"Dream?" John inquired as he lay next to her.

ci

"I actually dreamed of having sex with you," Karen began, "it was years ago, and I didn't even know that you were the one from the dream until recently"

"So, you can dream of the future?" John asked.

"Sometimes, although I don't always know what dreams may eventually come true," she replied, "I didn't know this one was even possible until now."

"What do you mean?" John asked.

"You are definitely blessed more than most men are down there," she spoke as she was looking just below John's waist.

"You have any plans for today?" John asked.

"No," Karen, replied, "what did you have in mind?"

"I'm planning to go for a hike."

"Sounds great"

Is this the End?

civ

Lightning Source UK Ltd.
Milton Keynes UK
UKHW040243060421
381484UK00001B/97